Truck Pals on the Job

Bobbi's Big Brake

written and illustrated by Ken Bowser

RED
CHAIR
•PRESS•™

Funny Bone Readers and Funny Bone Books are published by Red Chair Press
Red Chair Press LLC   PO Box 333   South Egremont, MA 01258-0333
www.redchairpress.com

For my Grandson, Liam Hayden Bowser
who never met a truck he didn't like.

Publisher's Cataloging-In-Publication Data
Bowser, Ken.

Bobbi's big brake / written and illustrated by Ken Bowser.

   pages : illustrations ; cm. -- (Funny bone readers. Truck pals on the job)

   Summary: All the big trucks stay busy with important work. Bobbi just wants to help,
but she is too small for the heavy lifting. With her self-esteem at a low point, will Bobbi
discover the important role she plays every day?

   Interest age level: 004-008.

   ISBN: 978-1-63440-062-6 (library hardcover)

   ISBN: 978-1-63440-063-3 (paperback)

   Issued also as an ebook. (ISBN: 978-1-63440-064-0)

   1. Trucks--Juvenile fiction. 2. Self-esteem--Juvenile fiction. 3. Friendship--Juvenile
fiction. 4. Trucks--Fiction. 5. Self-esteem--Fiction. 6. Friendship--Fiction. I. Title.

PZ7.B697 Bo 2016

[E]   2015937996

Printed in the United States of America
Distributed in the U.S. by Lerner Publisher Services. www.lernerbooks.com

1015 1P WRZSP16

The sun rose on the construction
site and Bobbi was up extra early.
"I'm going to help out at the
construction pit today," she said.

She asked Scoop, the front end loader if she could help. "Not today, Bobbi," she said. "You're far too small. You should go somewhere a little safer."

Big Bull the dozer was too busy
to talk. "Run along, Bobbi," he said.
"It's dangerous for someone so small
to be here."

Gil the giant dump truck wasn't any fun. "Bobbi! You're half the size of my wheels! I can't see you! Please go away," he scolded.

"Uncle T, can I help here?" she asked the tower crane. "I'm sorry, Bobbi. You're just too little. You should go over to the sandbox and out of the way."

Bobbi was tired of being told she was
too little. "You're too small!" they say.
"Run along!" "You're under foot!"
"Go away, Bobbi!" they say.

8

She went to the sandbox. "Why do I have to stay over here in this dumb old sandbox?" pouted Bobbi. "I wish there was a special job just for me."

The sun drifted lower and silence fell over the construction site for the day. The rumble of the big worker trucks faded and the site grew very still.

The next morning work began in the
construction pit just like every other day.
Movers moved, dozers dozed and the
pit grew deeper and deeper.

11

Bobbi watched as the bigger trucks worked. She was careful not to get too close to the edge of the pit as she had been told.

She loved to watch Big Bull the dozer work. He worked quickly and close to the edge of the pit. Big Bull always did a good job.

As Bobbi watched the big trucks work
she noticed something alarming. Some of
the sand and rocks at the edge of pit
were beginning to move and shift.

"This does not look safe," Bobbi thought
to herself. "Hey!" she yelled out to the
other trucks. "I think you should come
look at this!" They did not hear her.

"Hey, Guys!" she yelled again. "I don't think we should be so close to the edge of the pit right now!" she hollered. They still did not hear Bobbi's warning.

Just at that moment a huge boulder broke
free and began to roll right toward
Big Bull. "Bull can't hear my warnings!"
Bobbi thought. "I must do something!"

THUD!

Bobbi raced over and got right between Big Bull and the rolling boulder. She rammed herself into the boulder and applied her big front brakes just in time.

She held the boulder in place and sounded her giant horn. HOOOONK! Finally the other trucks heard her and escaped the dangerous rock slide just in time.

Rocks rumbled. Sand shifted and big boulders came crashing down into the pit but all of the trucks were safe thanks to Bobbi's keen eyes and loud warning.

"Bobbi you saved the entire crew," Big Bull shouted. "We would have been in big trouble without you, Bobbi. Your quick action and big brake saved the day!"

"Bobbi, we should never have doubted you," said Scoop the front end loader. "You performed the most important job of all today! You were being extra safe."

That same day Bobbi was named
Safety Chief and she was placed in
charge of keeping the entire site safe.
She even got a special hard hat!

Big Questions: Have you ever been told you were too young or too small to do something? How did it make you feel?

Big Words:

alarming: something to worry about

construction site: a place where things are being built

dozer: short for bulldozer, a machine that moves heavy things from one place to another and clears the ground